GIOVANNI MCGLONE

GUTSY G

RED

GIOVANNI MCGLONE

Gutsy G: Red
Copyright © 2021 Giovanni McGlone.

All rights reserved. No part of this book may be reproduced in any form or by any electronic or mechanical means, including information storage and retrieval systems, without permission in writing from the author, except by reviewers, who may quote brief passages in a review.

Contact gwhiz4christ@gmail.com for all inquiries.

I dedicate this book to people who are struggling with depression, anxiety, and mental illnesses. I dedicate this book to my roommate, because I had to forgive. Most of all, I dedicate this book to my family for being there and taking me in when I needed them the most! Thank you Jesus for sparing my life!

Hi! My name is Giovanni McGlone and this is my story. You can call me "GiGi", "G", or "Gutsy G". I made a plea to fight for justice and liberty in this world! I have special powers! I see things and hear things, but not just normal things. I can see time lapses in the timeline of lives and replays of the opposing forces. When I hear things, I have a radio station playing in my mind, with the full commentary.

Let's step back in time. "How did you get these powers?" you may ask. It all started in my freshman year of college. I was going to school to study graphic design. Until, one day, something happened that would change my life forever! I was sleeping on my bed, in my dormatory room, but for some reason, I woke up under a thick cloud of smoke in the air. I soon figured out that this smoke was the by-product of marijuana. An experiment gone wrong!

The second hand smoke had a lasting effect on my health, but also gave me my super abilities. Something in my brain was altered. Doctors and scientists around the world are still trying to figure out what part of the brain may have been affected to cause something like this to be able to happen to a person. Now, I can see into different realms and dimensions and I'm not the only one!

As I awakened from underneath the cloud of smoke, I could see animated smoke clouds under my eyelids. Not only that, but I started to see the color red everywhere, as if something, someone, or some entity was trying to tell me I was not in a safe zone or a safe place. Some people would classify my abilities as hallucinations. Others, would say, they are a God given gift. My powers took some getting used to! When my parents started noticing my abilities and eccentricity, I withdrew from the university that I was attending and moved back in with my parents.

My old room has now become my hideout and I now have a headquarters at un undisclosed location. At Gutsy G headquarters you can find top secret gadgets, gizmos, designs, blueprints, plans, missions, songs, instruments, and a top secret closet with all of my hero suits!

To this day, I'm still discovering my strengths and my weaknesses. At first, I was completely "out of it", to say the least. I had no idea what my body was going through and where this road would take me. Little did I know, this would become the beginning of a long, but rewarding journey.

Welcome to just one day in the life of a superhero with schizophrenia! Here's how it all began!

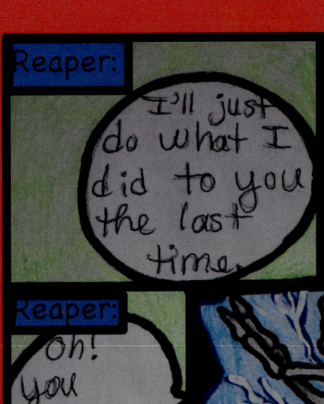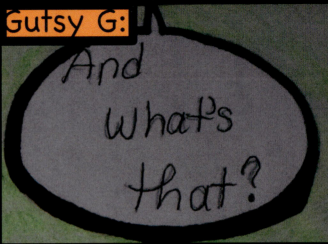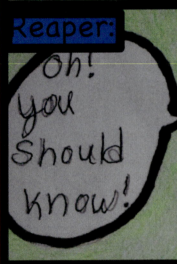

I fell to the floor.

I was feeling pain.

...pain in the gut!

I turned on the music in my headphones.

The song was saying, "No weapon formed against me shall prosper!"

Memory kicked in...

I had been hearing voices due to the mental illness...

I started singing...

I started reciting scripture...

It was just what I needed!

Like anyone with schizophrenia, I needed a little bit of encouragement!

Gutsy G:

I regained strength!

I stood to my feet!

I regained power...

I kept singing!

My hands began to glow red and green!

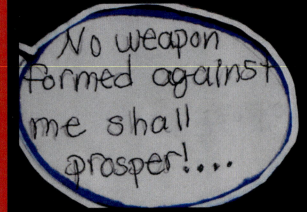

No weapon formed against me shall prosper!....

Reaper:

Gutsy G:

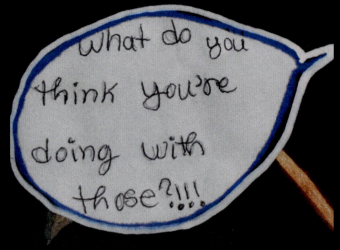

What do you think you're doing with those?!!!

He pointed his axe at me...

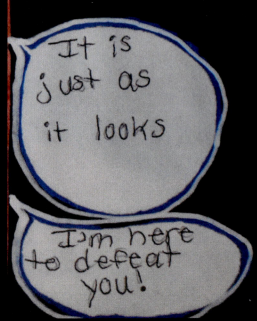

It is just as it looks

I'm here to defeat you!

After I blasted the reaper with my fists and the power of scripture through the Holy Spirit, the infamous reaper showed himself for who he truly was! He surely was a roaring lion!

He cried in agony as his powers diminished and he disappeared from my sight...

A portal opened before my eyes and a voice told me to go through it, for a portal is what brought the reaper here and a portal is what will take him back to where he belongs! So, I jumped through the portal.

And I landed on the moon!

When I landed on the moon, A figure in a white robe and sandals, threw to me, a ring to go on my finger.

On the ring, was the scripture Psalm 145:3...

The man told me,"The only way to close the portal, is by wearing the ring and reciting Psalm 145:3."

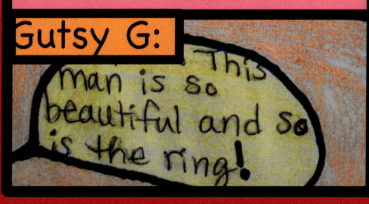

So, I jumped back through the portal to get to headquarters, with the ring still on my finger...

I took the ring and I called it the "Super Ring 2020" or the "SR 2020" for short.

I pointed the ring at the portal and recited the scripture just as I was told.

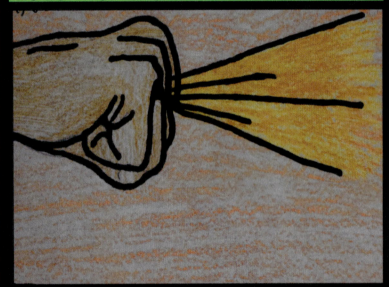

The portal closed and I was relieved to know that the reaper would no longer be able to torment me or the people of Earth!

And that was the end of him!

Gutsy G: By the power of Jesus Christ, the reaper is now defeated and peace has now come to the land!

Stay tuned...

for more of "Gutsy G"...

Although the reaper is gone, something tells me that this is not the end of adversity. Even scripture says that,"we will face troubles", but it also says to take heart, because Jesus has overcome the world! He overcame the world by dying on a cross for us. In hopes that we might accept his gift of eternal life. He was the sacrifice that paid for our sins. He is so great!

    I'm starting to wonder, just what else this ring can do! Maybe, I could use it to zap things. Maybe, I could use it to fly, but if there's one thing I know about rings, it's that they represent promises. I know that it can close portals, but what else is there to learn about it? Portals come in all shapes and sizes. Some portals lead us to bettering ourselves and some lead us to living a life of sin. For example, what you watch can be sinful and hurtful to God like; pornography, hypnosis, violence, and the list goes on and on! All of these things are sinful in God's eyes and according to his word. All of which, can be found using portals. When I say portals, I'm referring to the internet portals and our eyes, which are also like portals to our inner being. Some may even call our eyes "The windows to the soul".

    When we sin against God and take part in and view things like pornography, It harms us in a way that causes us to look at other people as objects instead of individuals, and with lust instead of love. A sinful life leads to death. Death is the payment for sin. But, a life lived according to God's will, leads to eternal life. Will you accept this gift today? If you said,"Yes!" your life will never be the same again! You must believe in your heart that Jesus raised from the dead and confess with your mouth that Jesus is Lord. Jesus now lives inside of you, his spirit will dwell with you and will help you along life's journeys! Whether it's hearing voices, or seeing things that no one else sees, I have hope that I can hold onto! Now, so do you! Through fire, through lions, through seas, through Giants, we will be unafraid! Hey, they don't call me "Gutsy G" for nothing!

NOTE FROM THE AUTHOR

Thank you so much for taking the time to read my book!

I would really appreciate it if you would:

Review this. If you enjoyed this story and work of art, consider leaving it a review. Reviews are helpful for up and coming authors. Every review truly means something special!

Share this. By sharing this book, whether it be on social media or by word-of-mouth, you will be sharing a message of love and hope, with those you cherish.

Connect. I'd love to connect with my readers. You can connect with me directly on Facebook, Twitter, YouTube, and Instagram at "@gwhiz4christ" or on Instagram at "@gutsygseries". You can also email me at "Gwhiz4Christ@gmail.com"

Thank you!

Made in the USA
Middletown, DE
09 September 2023